KT-220-586

Magic
Animal Friends

My name is

I celebrated World Book Day 2015
with this brilliant gift from my local
bookseller and Orchard Books!

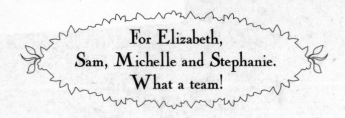

For Elizabeth,
Sam, Michelle and Stephanie.
What a team!

Special thanks to Valerie Wilding

ORCHARD BOOKS
338 Euston Road, London NW1 3BH
Orchard Books Australia
Level 17/207 Kent Street, Sydney, NSW 2000
A Paperback Original

First published in 2015 by Orchard Books

A CIP catalogue record for this book is available
from the British Library.

UK ISBN 978 1 40833 744 8
Export ISBN 978 1 40833 745 5

1 3 5 7 9 8 6 4 2

Printed in Great Britain
Orchard Books is an imprint of Hachette Children's Group and
published by The Watts Publishing Group Limited,
an Hachette UK company

www.hachette.co.uk

Lucy Longwhiskers
Finds a Friend

Daisy Meadows

ORCHARD

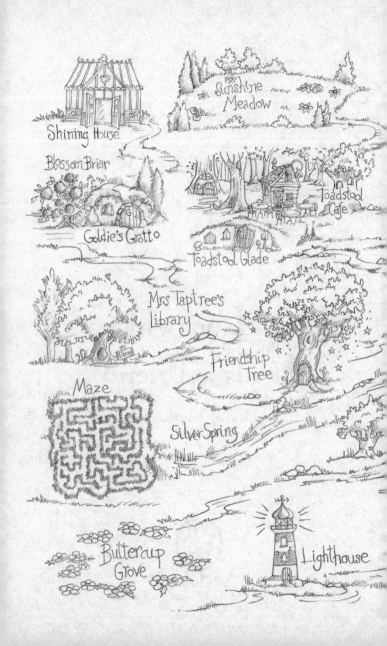

Shining House

Sunshine Meadow

Blossom Briar

Toadstool Cafe

Goldie's Grotto

Toadstool Glade

Mrs Taptree's Library

Friendship Tree

Maze

Silver Spring

Buttercup Grove

Lighthouse

Map of Friendship Forest

Ace Air Travel

Windmill

Mr Cleverfeather's Inventing Shed

Muddlepups' Den

Treasure Tree

Sparkly Falls

Featherbills' Barge

Waterwheel

Entrance to the Caverns

Swamp

Grizelda's Tower

Contents

CHAPTER ONE

The Friendship Tree

Lily Hart closed her book and sighed happily. "That was a brilliant story!"

Lily and her best friend, Jess Forester, were lying on the grass next to a rabbit pen in the warm afternoon sun. Lily's parents ran the Helping Paw Wildlife Hospital in a converted barn in their garden, and looked after all kinds of

 7

animals in need. All around them were pens full of little rabbits, guinea pigs, ducklings and fox cubs.

"I'll just finish my book," said Jess, "then we can swap."

Lily rolled over and found herself nose to nose with a little brown rabbit. He had a bandaged paw and was snuffling curiously through the wire fence.

Jess giggled. "I think he wants you to read him a story!"

"We've got lots of stories we could tell him!" said Lily. "All about the rabbits we've met in Friendship Forest!"

Jess and Lily shared a smile. Friendship Forest was their special secret. It was an amazing world where animals lived in little cottages, brightly painted dens, or even on boats. And every one of them could talk!

Lily poked a dandelion leaf through the wire. The rabbit nibbled it, then looked up, his ears twitching.

"What is it?" Lily asked softly, turning to look.

A beautiful golden cat, with eyes as green as fresh mint leaves, bounded across the grass.

"It's Goldie!" Jess cried.

The cat purred and rubbed her face against Jess's chin, then against Lily's. Then she mewed and turned towards Brightley Stream, at the bottom of Lily's garden.

"She wants to take us back to Friendship Forest," said Jess, closing her book. "We're going to have another adventure!"

They hurried after Goldie, across the stream and towards the Friendship Tree, in the middle of Brightley Meadow.

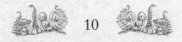

The tree looked dead but, as Goldie drew near, bright green leaves and beautiful blossoms sprang into life all over it. A song thrush perched on the topmost branch and sang joyfully as butterflies danced among the colourful flowers below.

Goldie touched a paw to the trunk and words magically appeared, carved into the bark.

The girls felt a flutter of excitement as together they read the words out loud: "Friendship Forest!"

Immediately, a small door with a leaf-shaped handle appeared in the trunk. Jess opened it, and light spilled out.

11

As Goldie darted through the doorway, the girls grabbed hold of each other's hands.

"Isn't this exciting?" said Lily, stepping into the shimmering light.

Once they were inside, they tingled all over as they shrank, just a little.

As the golden glow faded, Jess and Lily found themselves in a sun-dappled forest clearing. The scent of candyfloss flowers and dandyrose buds filled the warm air. Colourful curtains billowed at tiny windows in the trunks of tall trees, and cosy little cottages nestled in the roots below.

Nearby, waiting for the girls, was

 12

Goldie. Now they were in Friendship Forest she was standing upright, as tall as their shoulders, and wearing a glittery scarf.

She ran to hug them. "Welcome back!" she cried.

"It's so lovely to be able to talk to you again," said Lily.

"And to be back in Friendship Forest," Jess added. "Oh look!" she said as a tiny mouse scurried past, clutching a book. "There's Molly Twinkletail!"

Then Mrs Featherbill the duck waddled through the trees with a book tucked beneath her wing. Her eight ducklings followed close behind, each carrying a little book as well. Ellie Featherbill, the youngest, fluffiest duckling, waved at the girls and Goldie before hurrying after her family.

"What is going on?" Lily asked curiously.

Goldie smiled. "It's Story Day in Friendship Forest!"

"Story Day!" said Jess. "What's that?"

"It's the day that we get new books here in the forest," Goldie explained. "All our books are made magically by the Book Tree. It only makes them on Story Day, when its leaves come out."

Jess and Lily looked at each other. "That sounds amazing!"

But Goldie glanced around with a worried expression.

"What's wrong?" Lily asked.

"I thought I heard someone cackling this morning," said Goldie. "That's why I came to get you."

Lily gasped. "Grizelda?"

"Oh no!" said Jess, putting her arm
around the cat. The wicked witch
wanted to take over Friendship Forest
and ruin it for all the animals.

"If Grizelda's here it can only mean
one thing." Goldie turned to them
anxiously. "She's going to try to spoil
Story Day!"

CHAPTER TWO

Book Tree Magic

"If Grizelda tries any of her nasty tricks," Jess said fiercely, "we'll be ready to stop her."

Lily nodded. "We've broken her horrid spells before, and we'll do it again," she said. "We won't let her harm Friendship Forest."

"Thank you," said Goldie. "We're so

lucky that you're our friends. Come on, I'll show you what happens here on Story Day!"

Jess and Lily shared an excited glance and followed the cat through the forest.

An elderly owl wearing a monocle and a waistcoat hurried towards them, holding a pile of books in his wings.

"Less and Jilly!" he cried, muddling his words as usual. "I mean, Jess and Lily. And Goldie, too!"

"Hello, Mr Cleverfeather," said Jess.

"Where are you going?" asked Lily.

"To Mrs Taptree the woodpecker's library," he said. "The Book Tree has just made these lovely boo nooks – I mean new books. Look!"

He showed them two books. One was called *Great Owl Inventions* and the other was *A Hundred Uses for Old Feathers*.

"They look interesting – especially if you're an owl!" Lily giggled. Then she looked serious. "But watch out for Grizelda, Mr Cleverfeather," she said. "We think she's going to try to ruin Story Day."

The owl nodded. "I'll keep my pies sealed – I mean, my eyes peeled," he said, and hurried on.

Goldie led the girls to a clearing with a huge tree in the middle. Its trunk was covered in silvery letters and all its leaves were white, like pieces of paper. Lots of young animals were gathered around the tree, plucking the leaves then busily scribbling on them.

"That's the Book Tree," said Goldie. "Watch what happens when someone finishes writing a story."

A little squirrel jumped up. "All done!" she said, putting her leaf inside a hollow in the trunk.

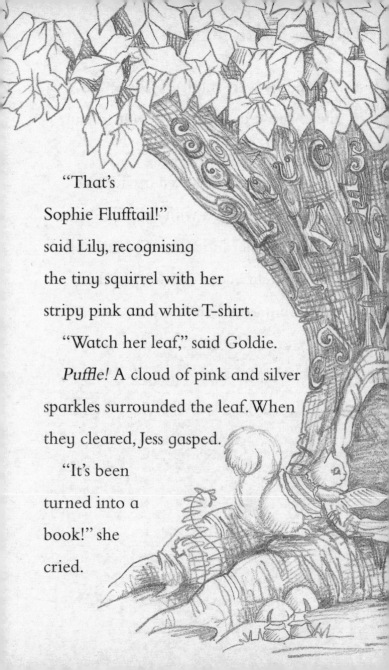

"That's
Sophie Flufftail!"
said Lily, recognising
the tiny squirrel with her
stripy pink and white T-shirt.

"Watch her leaf," said Goldie.

Puffle! A cloud of pink and silver
sparkles surrounded the leaf. When
they cleared, Jess gasped.

"It's been
turned into a
book!" she
cried.

The pages were made of leaves and the cover said *The Magic Nut Tree* in swirling green letters.

Sophie Flufftail picked up her book and bounced with delight. She added it to her little pile of books and immediately began writing another story on a fresh leaf.

"We can't let Grizelda spoil Story Day – the animals are having such fun," said Lily.

"All except one." Jess pointed to a little rabbit. "Look! Lucy Longwhiskers seems worried."

The tiny rabbit's ears were drooping sadly as she stared down at her leaf. When the girls approached, she looked up and gave them a wobbly smile.

"What's wrong?" asked Lily.

"I can't think of anything to write about," Lucy said in a rush, "and the magic only works on Story Day and I might not think of an idea in time to make a book and everyone else has got

 23

lots of ideas and – and…"

She sat down sadly with her chin in her paws.

Jess stroked Lucy gently. "Why don't you ask one of the others to help you? It looks like Sophie Flufftail has lots of ideas."

"But I don't know Sophie very well," Lucy said, glancing at the squirrel shyly. Sophie was curled around her leaf, her tail swishing happily as she wrote. "Besides," Lucy added, "I think she's too busy to help."

At this, Sophie's ears pricked up. She bounded over and hugged the girls, then turned to Lucy. "I'd love to help you!" she said. "Reading other stories always gives me ideas if I'm stuck. Perhaps you could do that?"

"Good plan!" said Lily. "Let's go to Mrs Taptree's library and look at some of the books there."

"Ooh, yes," said Lucy. She smiled at the squirrel. "Thank you, Sophie." The little rabbit thought for a minute. "Do you want to come, too?" she added.

"Yes, please!" Sophie grinned.

They set off, following Goldie through the trees.

"Sophie, what's your new story about?" Lucy asked.

"It's called *The Golden Squirrel…*" Sophie began.

As the two little animals chattered, Goldie whispered to Lily and Jess. "It's so nice that they're making friends! But we have to remember to watch out for Grizelda."

"I've got my pies sealed," joked Jess.

Goldie stopped at a big tree with a door set into the trunk. Through the windows, they could glimpse tall shelves filled with books.

"Mrs Taptree's library!" said Jess.

Goldie was about to knock, when Lily gave a cry. "Look out!"

An orb of yellow-green light floated towards them, and burst in a shower of smelly green sparks. In its place stood a tall, bony woman with wild green hair, a purple tunic, black trousers and sharply pointed high-heeled boots.

Jess gasped. "Grizelda!"

CHAPTER THREE

Grizelda's Evil Spell

Lucy Longwhiskers trembled as the witch stamped her foot. Sophie scampered up into Lily's arms and covered her eyes with her tail.

"I hate books!" Grizelda shrieked. "I hate stories and I hate Story Day! I'm going to make sure that no one has any fun today!"

Jess picked Lucy up and held her close. "That's a horrible thing to say, Grizelda!" she yelled.

"Too bad!" the witch said with a sneer. "Because I've got a plan."

Lily groaned.

Grizelda pointed her bony finger at a dandyrose bush growing near the library tree. Dirty yellow sparks shot towards it as Grizelda muttered,

"Make this plant be really clever,

Stop nasty stories for ever and ever!"

With one last cackle, Grizelda snapped her fingers and disappeared in another shower of stinky sparks.

"Look what's happening!" cried Lily

 30

as the dandyrose began to change.
Long, curling black vines sprouted
out from where the beautiful flowers
had been. The
girls watched in
dismay as the vines
grew longer and
stronger. They twined
around and around
the library tree trunk,
criss-crossing over the
doors and windows,
sealing them shut.

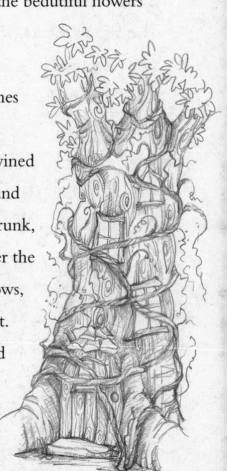

The frightened
faces of Mrs
Taptree and

her two chicks, Dig and Tipper, peered
through the top window. Behind them
was Mr Cleverfeather.

"Let us out! Quick! Quick!" Mrs
Taptree squawked.

Mr Cleverfeather gave a shaky hoot.

But the vines continued to coil around the library until the window was completely covered.

"Oh no," said Jess with a gasp of horror. "They're trapped!"

Lily cupped her hands around her mouth. "We'll get you out somehow!" she shouted. "Don't be scared!"

Jess started tugging at the vines, trying to tear them away. "They're too tough!" she cried. "What are we going to do?"

"We need a spell to get rid of the vines," said Goldie. "But all the spell books are inside the library. This is dreadful!"

"Poor Mrs Taptree and poor Dig and Tipper," Lucy sniffed. "Poor Mr Cleverfeather."

"There must be something we can do," said Sophie bravely. "We have to save the stories!"

"Stories…" Jess said to herself. "That's it! You clever squirrel! Grizelda's spell didn't mention the library. It was about stopping *stories*. The vines are growing over the library because of the stories inside. But maybe if there were stories out here, the vines would grow near them instead?"

"Then we can run into the library and get a spell book!" Lily exclaimed.

Goldie nodded. "All we need are some stories."

"But where will we get some?" Sophie said with a sigh.

"I've had an idea!" cried Lucy, her long ears twitching. "Sophie's books!

We can use those. She's really good at writing stories."

"That's a great idea, Lucy! Let's try it!" said Lily. She glanced at the library, where the vines were now so thick that she couldn't see their friends through the windows. "But we'd better hurry!"

CHAPTER FOUR

Sophie Flufftail's Stories

Jess raced back from the Book Tree, clutching Sophie's books. She handed one each to Lily, Goldie, Lucy and Sophie.

"Do you think it'll work?" Sophie asked, her eyes wide with worry.

"I don't know," said Jess, "but

 37

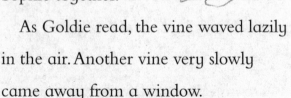

we've got to try."

Goldie opened her book. "I'll start," she said. "Once upon a time, there was a little nut tree…"

A vine twitched. Slowly, it peeled away from the library.

"It's working!" squealed Lucy and Sophie together.

As Goldie read, the vine waved lazily in the air. Another vine very slowly came away from a window.

"Yes, it's working," said Lily, "but it's taking far too long! We've got to save the Taptrees and Mr Cleverfeather."

"I know!" said Jess. "Let's all read all at once – maybe that will speed it up."

"Good idea!" said Lily. "Ready? All together, READ!"

Even though they were doing something so important, Lily and Jess almost giggled at the dreadful noise they made with their mixed-up stories. There were squirrel princesses jumbled up with magic boxes and lost toys and naughty pixies!

Suddenly, one of the vines flew away from the library, twisting as it lunged towards them.

Lucy jumped back with a frightened

squeak, her little white
tail quivering.

"Keep back, everyone!"
called Jess.

Sophie bounded to Lucy's
side, and held her paw. "I'll
stay with you. We'll be fine!"

They carried on reading,
and more vines tore
themselves away from

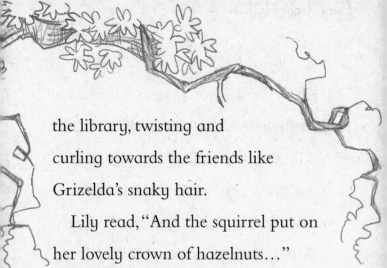

the library, twisting and

curling towards the friends like

Grizelda's snaky hair.

Lily read, "And the squirrel put on

her lovely crown of hazelnuts…"

"The dragon sneezed so hard,"

read Lucy as she clutched Sophie's paw,

"he flew backwards, then…"

A vine swooped towards the little

rabbit and tried to grab her book.

Sophie pulled Lucy away and the vine

made a dive for Goldie's book instead.

The cat leaped back.

"Look!" Jess cried as the vines came

away from the library door. "Lily, you're closest – you can run inside now! Everyone else keep reading!"

Lily dodged around the waving vines. She opened the library door and ducked inside.

Mrs Taptree and Mr Cleverfeather rushed over to her, their wings flapping in alarm. Dig and Tipper peeked out from behind a ladder.

"I knew you'd sum and cave us," said Mr Cleverfeather as he smoothed his feathers. "I mean, come and save us."

Lily searched the shelves. "We're not safe yet," she said, glancing outside to where the vines were getting closer and closer to her friends.

Sophie, Goldie, Lucy and Jess were reading bravely, but their voices were getting high and panicky as the vines reached through the air towards them.

"We need a spell to get rid of those vines," she said.

"Quick! Quick! I know just the thing," said Mrs Taptree. She took a book down and

gave it to Lily. "It's called *Plant Magic.*
Quick! Quick!"

"Lily!" Jess yelled from outside.
"Hurry!"

Through the door, Lily could see that
one of the vines had wrapped around
Jess's arm!

She flicked desperately through the
pages, but it was no good. "I can't find
the right spell!" she cried.

CHAPTER FIVE

Forest Friends

Mr Cleverfeather flapped his wings. "Look at the burst stage, Lily!" he cried with an eager hoot. "It'll have a list of all the bells in the spook!"

Lily shook her head in confusion. *What did Mr Cleverfeather mean?* But then she realised. "Oh! The first page lists the spells in the book!"

A moment later, she had found what she needed – a spell to make weeds disappear.

"Let's go!" she cried.

They hurried outside, ducking beneath the writing vines. Another vine had wrapped around Jess's leg, and vines were coiled around Goldie's paw and one of Lucy's long ears, too. Sophie gave a squeal as a vine snatched her by her fluffy tail.

"Lily!" Jess yelled. "Thank goodness! Have you got a spell?"

"Yes," Lily called. "I just need to change a few words…" She quickly thought, then took a deep breath.

 46

"Listen, vines, to what I say,

Now's the time to go away.

Shrivel up and leave the tree,

Set Mrs Taptree's library free!"

"Brilliant, Lily!" cried Goldie.

But nothing seemed to be happening.

The vines were still holding onto Jess, Goldie and the little animals.

"Oh no," groaned Lily. "It's not going to work."

But then the vine around Lucy's ear started to move.

"Yay!" cried Sophie, as the vine around her tail fell away. The vines started to shrink, faster and faster. In a few moments, the last of them disappeared back into the dandyrose bush. There was a puff of petals, and the bush returned to normal.

"Hooray!" cried Dig and Tipper.

Mrs Taptree clapped her wingtips. "You've saved my library!"

Mr Cleverfeather hooted with happiness. "You've saved Dory Stay, too!" he said. "I mean…"

Everybody laughed.

"We know what you mean!" said Jess. The friends joined hands, paws and

wings in a circle and danced for joy.

As they whirled and skipped, Lily

caught sight of something floating

through the trees – a familiar, horrible

yellow-green orb of light!

"Grizelda!" she cried.

Everyone huddled together as the
orb exploded into smelly, spitting
sparks.

The witch appeared, shaking her fist.
Her green hair whipped around her
head like angry snakes. "You interfering
girls may have won
this time, but I'll
be back," she
shrieked. "And
my magic will
be more powerful
than ever! Just you
wait!"

She snapped her fingers and disappeared in another burst of sparks.

The girls held Goldie's paws.

"We'll always be ready to help stop Grizelda's plans," said Jess.

The cat hugged them. "I know you will," she said. "Friendship Forest is so lucky to have you."

The girls hugged Goldie, then smiled as they saw Sophie Flufftail and Lucy Longwhiskers hugging too.

"Getting to know you has been really fun," said Lucy.

"It's so nice to have a new friend," said Sophie with a smile. "*And* I know what you can write your story about."

Lucy looked puzzled.

"Our adventure with Lily and Jess!" cried Sophie.

Lucy gave a squeak of delight, and hugged Sophie so hard that the little squirrel's tail shook.

"That's brilliant!" Lucy said. "Will you help me write it?"

"Of course!" said Sophie. "Making

friends with you has made this the best
Story Day ever!"

Goldie and the girls said goodbye
to Mrs Taptree and Mr Cleverfeather.
Then they followed Lucy and Sophie
back to the Book Tree. Lucy and
Sophie set to work writing their story,
and when they'd finished, Lucy put
their leaves under the Book Tree.

Puffle!

Pink and silver sparkles surrounded
the leaves. When they cleared, Lucy
gasped, "My book!" She ran to pick
it up. "Look at the cover!" she cried.
My Story Day Adventure was written
on the cover above a picture of Lucy,

 54

Sophie, Goldie and the girls.

"Wow!" said Lily. "Goldie, maybe Mrs Taptree would like Lucy's book for her library?"

The cat smiled. "I'm sure she would."

A leaf dropped from the Book Tree. Then another fell,

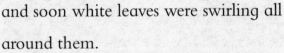

and soon white leaves were swirling all around them.

"Story Day is over for another year," Goldie said.

"I can't wait until the next one," Sophie said with a grin.

"Me neither," said Jess. She kneeled to hug Sophie and Lucy. "But for now it's time we went home."

The bunny rabbit and squirrel stretched up to hug them both goodbye.

The girls waved to their animal friends, then followed Goldie back to the Friendship Tree.

The cat touched her paw to the trunk, and the door appeared. She hugged the girls close. "Thank you both. I'll come and see you very soon," she promised.

The girls stepped through the door into golden, shimmering light. They felt the tingle that meant they were returning to their proper size, then the light faded and they were back in Brightley Meadow.

"Wow!" said Jess, as they ran back to the wildlife hospital. Their books were still lying on the grass and the animals were still hopping around in their enclosures. The little brown rabbit had put his nose through the wire fence, and was nibbling the corner of Jess's book. It was as if they'd never been away!

"What an adventure!" said Lily.

"It was amazing," agreed Jess. "In fact, it was just like something out of a story!"

The End

'Tons of fun!'
Meg Cabot, author of *The Princess Diaries*

If you like **Magic Animal Friends**,
you'll like **What Ever After!**
Turn over for a sneak peak of the new book
by Sarah Mlynowski,

I look around the cottage at all the small furniture.

I think about the apple and the woman in disguise.

The stepmum in disguise.

'You're Snow White?' I ask again. She nods.

'The real Snow White?'

'I think so. Unless there's another Snow White?'

'I think you're it,' Jonah says.

'But…' I slump back in my tiny chair, the gears of my brain turning.

Snow White exists only in a fairy tale. That means that if the Snow White here is the real Snow White, then we,

Jonah and I, are also in a…in a…
It makes no sense. You don't just
fall through a mirror and land in a
fairy tale.

'We're in the story,' Jonah says. 'It's
magic!'

'But there's no such thing as magic,'
I say. 'Not in the real world.'

'Maybe there is.'

'But…but…' I strain to come up
with an argument that will convince
him. I mean, me. I mean, him!

'You know how you want to be a
judge when you grow up?' Jonah asks,
his tone annoyingly calm.

'Why yes, I do know that. What does

that have to do with anything?'

He shrugs. 'Judges look at the evidence, right?'

I'm silent.

'So look at the evidence,' he says.

I don't want to. But I do. I study the girl in front of me:

- Black hair.

- Pale skin.

- Red lips.

Just like in the story.

Read

WHAT Ever After

FAIREST OF ALL

to find out what happens next!

Magic
Animal Friends

Read all the Magic Animal Friends adventures and be part of the secret!

Series One

Series Two

3 stories in 1!

www.magicanimalfriends.com

Magic
Animal Friends

Can you keep the secret?

There's lots of fun for everyone at
www.magicanimalfriends.com

Play games and explore the secret world of
Friendship Forest, where animals can talk!

Join the
Magic Animal Friends Club!

Special competitions

Exclusive content

All the latest Magic Animal Friends news!

To join the Club, simply go to

www.magicanimalfriends.com/join-our-club/